Trash
to
Treasure

Wendy Perkinson

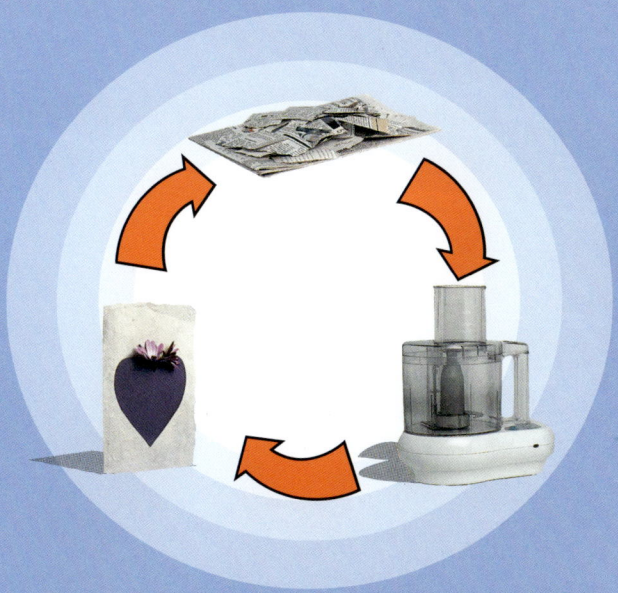

photographs by Matt Grace

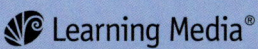 Learning Media®

For many years, we used paper only once and then buried it, burned it, or dumped it in the ocean. Now, we're beginning to understand how harmful this is. By reusing and recycling paper, we can cut down on the amount of waste and damage to the environment.

We can all help. We can start by using less paper and by choosing to use recycled paper. Look around for the recycle logo, which tells you what can be recycled and what has been made using recycled paper.

Make use of curbside collections and drop-off centers. The paper they collect is transported to a processing plant where it is made into new paper products. The good news is that paper can be recycled over and over again.

Recycling paper is a good thing you can do at home. It's easy, fun, and messy! The paper you can make is excellent for turning into greeting cards. Best of all, it's almost free!

You'll need:

▶ A food processor
▶ An iron
▶ Two sheets of newspaper torn into pieces about the size of your hand
▶ Three cups of water
▶ Two large spoonfuls of white or clear glue
▶ A large tub filled finger-deep with water
▶ The legs cut from three pairs of old tights
▶ Some wire coat hangers
▶ Tape and scissors
▶ Pliers.

Stretch out one of the coat hangers and bend it into a square using the pliers. Tape around the wire where the two ends meet. Now carefully stretch one leg of the tights over the square. Make sure that it is tight and flat. Tie a knot at each end of the tights leg. This is the frame to make your sheet of paper. You'll need to make around five frames.

Put one handful of the paper and some of the water into the food processor. Close the lid and turn the food processor onto high. Keep adding the paper slowly, along with more of the water, until you have a sloppy gray paper pulp.

When you have added all the paper and all three cups of water, leave the machine on for another two minutes.

Stir the glue into the tub of water. Add the pulp. Use your hands to stir everything until it is well mixed. Scoop a frame into the bottom of the tub. Lift it up very slowly, making sure that the frame is flat, to catch some paper pulp. Count to twenty as you lift the frame out, letting all of the extra water drain off.

Repeat the scooping and draining steps with the other frames until all the pulp has been used.

Put the frames in a warm place to dry. When they are completely dry, you can peel off your paper.

You can reuse the frames many times.

Iron your new pieces of paper and trim them to a shape that you like. Fold them in half, decorate the front of each card, and write a message inside. Well done! You've made a treasure from trash, and you've helped to save a tree!